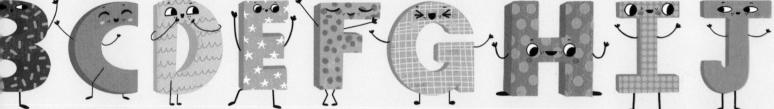

THE
OLPHABET

"O" NO!
AN ALPHABET REVOLT

by Jess M. Brallier

Illustrated by Nichola Cowdery

RP|KIDS
PHILADELPHIA

Beth Wolfensberger Singer was first to kindly welcome my story of "O" and then brilliantly imagine how it might look. I'm blessed with Beth's generous support, thoughtful work, welcomed imagination, and most of all, her friendship.

For Ruby
who inspires and makes me smile.
I'm so proud and forever grateful.
—JB

To my gorgeous family, Sean, Maggie and Hendrix.
Thanks for being awesome!
—NC

Running Press Kids
Hachette Book Group
1290 Avenue of the Americas, New York, NY 10104
www.runningpress.com/rpkids
@RP_Kids

Printed in China

First Edition: May 2021

Published by Running Press Kids, an imprint of Perseus Books, LLC, a subsidiary of Hachette Book Group, Inc. The Running Press Kids name and logo is a trademark of the Hachette Book Group.

The Hachette Speakers Bureau provides a wide range of authors for speaking events. To find out more, go to www.hachettespeakersbureau.com or call (866) 376-6591.

The publisher is not responsible for websites (or their content) that are not owned by the publisher.

Print book cover and interior design by Marissa Raybuck.

Library of Congress Control Number: 2019956376

ISBNs: 978-0-7624-9820-8 (hardcover), 978-0-7624-9819-2 (ebook), 978-0-7624-7108-9 (ebook), 978-0-7624-7107-2 (ebook)

APS

10 9 8 7 6 5 4 3 2 1

I'm the letter O.
Always in the middle.

Why can't I be first in the alphabet?
Instead of **A**.
I'm a simple circle.
Easy to write.

I'd be a friendly welcome to the alphabet.
I'm already a leader of letters.

One, Oodles, Orange, Octopus.

Plus "O baby," "O boy," and "O, say can you see?"

And that **A-B-C** song sounds even better as **O-B-C**.
Go ahead, sing it. "**O, B, C, D, E, F, G . . .**"
Omazing, right?

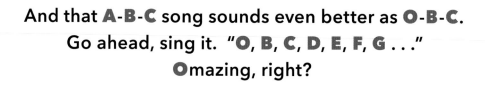

At the alphabet's front, I'd be far from **Q**.
My tailed twin who only likes to play with **U**.

QUack!
QUick!
QUiet!
QUeen!

I should at least be next to **K**.
We like being together.

People are **OK** with that.

Or beside **X**.
We hug and kiss. **XOXO**.

And play tic-tac-toe.

Maybe I could follow G. Together, we make things GO!

Yet, **N** and **P** keep me safe,
being sure I don't roll too far.

If first in the alphabet,
I might roll away and get lost.
O no!

And would it really be as much fun up by B?
Maybe not.
B can be Boring, Bossy, Bad,
and talks nonstop . . . Blah Blah Blah!

BLAH!
BLAH!
BLAH

STUFF TO TALK ABOUT

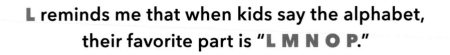

L reminds me that when kids say the alphabet,
their favorite part is "L M N O P."

We're five fun letters.
It would be sad to break us up.

N says she'd miss me.
Together we talk like grown-ups.

NO! NOpe! **NO**t yet!

Poor **P** pouts.
Says it won't be the same without me.
"I've been after **O** forever."

I feel the same way,
imagining me way up the line,
far from my friends.

Come to think of it,
why be in a line at all?
And not a circle?

We'd look like me!
We could be . . . the **O**lphabet.

It wouldn't matter who is first
As there's no start or end to a circle.
Maybe that's better. More fair.

Z no longer always stuck at the end.

A not showing-off up front.

And I'd still be with best friends.
Where I'm wanted.

o my.
o gosh.
o no.

Now that I think about it
even more . . .

I'm not moving!
I'm happy just where I am!